Mystery
of the
Rusty
Key

Mystery
of the
Rusty
Key

BY JANELLE DILLER
ILLUSTRATIONS BY ADAM TURNER

Published by WorldTrek Publishing

Copyright © 2018 by Pack-n-Go Girls

Printed in the USA

Pack-n-Go Girls® is a trademark of Pack-n-Go Girls. All rights reserved. No part
of this book may be reproduced or utilized in any form or by any means, electronic
or mechanical, including photocopying, recording, or by any information storage or
retrieval system, without permission in writing from the publisher. Inquiries should be
addressed to WorldTrek Publishing, 121 East Vermijo, Colorado Springs, CO 80903.

Visit our website at www.packngogirls.com.

This is a work of fiction. Names, characters, places, and incidents either are the product
of the author's imagination or are used fictitiously. If you head to Australia, make sure
you spend some time in Sydney. It's a wonderful place to visit. Any other resemblance
to actual events, locales, organizations, or persons, living or dead, is entirely coincidental
and beyond the intent of either the author or the publisher.

Illustrations by Adam Turner

ISBN 978-1-936376-58-2

Cataloging-in-Publication Data available from the Library of Congress.

To sweet Georgia, the newest Pack-n-Go Girl to forever steal my heart. Know what's important to you. Take risks to follow your dreams.

Mystery of the Rusty Key is the second book in the Pack-n-Go Girls Australia adventures. The first book, *Mystery of the Min Min Lights* tells how Wendy and Chloe meet. Here's a bit about the book:

> It's hot. It's windy. It's dusty. It's the Australian outback. Wendy Lee arrives from California. She's lucky to meet Chloe Taylor, who invites Wendy to their sheep station. It sounds like fun except that someone is stealing the sheep. And the thief just might be something as crazy as a UFO.

Contents

Meet the Characters

Wendy Lee

is spending six months in Australia. She's glad to meet Chloe and have a new friend.

Chloe Taylor

loves their sheep station. Now she gets to share Sydney with her new friend, Wendy.

Jack Taylor

is Chloe's brother. He's turning six in just two days. He's excited to spend his birthday in Sydney.

Mrs. Taylor

is Chloe and Jack's mum. She's a little nervous about seeing her aunty again after almost 30 years.

Aunty Pauline

is Mrs. Taylor's aunty. She's discovered a letter that's been lost for over 100 years.

What will the

The Rusty Key

unlock?

And now, the mystery begins . . .

Chapter 1

The Right House

"Is this the right house?" Chloe asked her mom.

"I don't know." Mrs. Taylor tapped her fingers on the steering wheel.

This made Wendy nervous. She'd been excited to come to Sydney, Australia, with her friend Chloe and Chloe's mom and brother, Jacko. Now that they were here, though, she wasn't so sure. There was something going on and Wendy couldn't quite figure it out.

"Is this the right address?" Chloe asked her

mom. "317 Jacaranda Street?"

"Yes."

"Then why isn't it the right house?" Jacko asked his mom.

"I don't know. I don't remember that it looked like this," Mrs. Taylor said.

The four of them stared at the house. The broad front porch, or *verandah* as Chloe called it, ran the length of the two-story white house. Brilliant purple jacaranda trees stood at each end of the *verandah*. They exploded with color. The trees' horn-shaped flowers hung in full bunches from even the smallest branches. A wild hedge of lavender grew along the *verandah* and the sidewalk, or *footpath*. In spite of the cheery color, something about the house looked sad to Wendy. Maybe it was the missing roof shingles. Maybe it was the sagging *verandah*. Maybe it was the broken front step. The house looked like it hadn't been painted in years, maybe decades.

The Right House

"When were you here last?" Chloe asked her mom.

"A long time ago. Twenty years ago. No, probably thirty," Mrs. Taylor said. "I was close to your age, Chloe. We were visiting my great-aunty Margaret."

"But your great-aunty passed away, right?" Chloe said. "Now we're here to see your aunty Pauline, right?"

"Yes," Mrs. Taylor said. "But that was also the last time I saw Aunty Pauline, too."

"Huh?" Jacko said. "Why haven't you seen her in so long?"

Mrs. Taylor tapped the steering wheel some more. "It's a long story. We had a *bit of a blue.*" She looked at Wendy. "An argument, I mean. Soon after that visit, Great-Aunty Margaret died and Aunty Pauline moved to England. We lost touch."

"But didn't you email each other? Weren't you

friends on Facebook?" Chloe asked.

Mrs. Taylor laughed. "That was long before Facebook and way before we used email. I don't know if Aunty Pauline uses email today. Probably not."

"But then how did you know she was back in Sydney?" Chloe asked.

"The old-fashioned way," Mrs. Taylor said and smiled. "Snail mail."

"Snail mail?" Jacko asked. "What's that?"

"That's a letter with a stamp on it that comes in the mail."

"Doesn't that take forever?" Jacko asked.

"Yes," Mrs. Taylor said. She took a deep breath. "But that's why we're here now. Aunty Pauline asked us to come. She said she'd found something really important."

"What did she find?" Chloe asked.

Mrs. Taylor stared at the house. "I guess we'll find out."

The Right House

The four of them got out of the car. Wendy broke into a sweat from the blast of hot, muggy air. She tucked a strand of her straight black hair behind her ear. She wiped her forehead. Mrs. Taylor's, Chloe's, and Jacko's curly blond hair looked even curlier.

Nobody seemed to have very much courage. Wendy couldn't figure out just why. But since they were nervous, that made Wendy nervous. She chewed her thumbnail.

They paraded up the broken concrete walk to the front steps. The house looked even shabbier up close. The *verandah* boards needed paint, at least the ones that weren't broken. Cobwebs strung from every corner. A gray film covered the windows. They hadn't been washed in years. Dusty curtains hung from the windows by the front door. One of the curtains moved slightly as they reached the last step.

Before Mrs. Taylor could ring the bell, the weathered door swung open. A shrunken old woman poked her head out. She'd tried to pull her curly gray hair into a bun, but most of it seemed to be falling out. Her steel-blue eyes darted from one person to the next. "You must be Laura," she said to Mrs. Taylor. Her raspy voice sounded harsh. "I'm glad you got my letter. It's good to see you again finally." She didn't sound happy at all.

The Right House

"Hello, Aunty Pauline," Mrs. Taylor said. "I'm glad to see you, too, after all these years." It sounded forced to Wendy, not friendly like Mrs. Taylor usually sounded.

The old lady opened the door wider but didn't invite them in. Instead, she cocked her head to one side and studied the three children. "You have three children." It wasn't a question. She stared at Wendy.

Wendy giggled nervously. She knew what the old lady was thinking. With her straight black hair and olive skin, she looked the opposite of Chloe and Jacko, who had blond curly hair and freckled faces.

"Just two," Mrs. Taylor said. She gently pushed her children forward a bit. "This is Chloe and Jacko. Chloe is nine, and Jacko will be six in two days." Then she put her hands on Wendy's shoulders. Wendy felt a tiny bit calmer. "And this is Wendy Lee, Chloe's friend. She's from California. But she's living in Australia for six months while her mother is doing a software project at one of the local mining companies near Port Augusta. We thought it would be fun for her to see Sydney."

The ancient woman tilted her head again and then finally shuffled back a bit and opened the door wider. "I'm glad to see you brought the boy with you," she said and then sighed deeply.

Chloe and Wendy looked at Jacko. His eyes narrowed.

The woman grumbled to herself then muttered, "Come in, come in." She leaned down to Jacko and patted the top of his head. "I have a letter for you. It's from your great-great-great-grandfather."

"My what?" Jacko looked at his mom. He raised his eyebrows. "Who?"

Mrs. Taylor pulled him close. "What do you mean, Aunty Pauline?" Her voice squeaked nervously.

But the old woman only shuffled away. She knew a secret, and she didn't intend to share it. *"She'll be right,"* Aunty Pauline said, which meant no worries.

Wendy's stomach twisted into a knot. How could Aunty Pauline act like there was nothing to worry about when there was everything to worry about? After all, it wasn't every day you got a letter from someone you'd never met who had been dead for over a hundred years.

Chapter 2

The Rusty Key

"What does she mean there's a letter for me?" Jacko whispered to the girls. "How can there be a letter for me from someone I've never met?"

"I don't know, Jacko," Chloe whispered back.

"And he's a *dead* someone." Jacko shuddered.

Chloe gritted her teeth. "The whole thing is pretty weird to me." She grabbed Jacko's hand. Jacko grabbed Wendy's hand. The three of them followed Mrs. Taylor into the living room. Their hearts pounded. Their palms felt sweaty.

A couple of threadbare couches and four shabby chairs cluttered the living room. The whole place felt stuffy. Too much warm, stale air filled the room. Wendy sniffed. It smelled musty, like the windows and doors had been shut for decades. At least the old woman had cleaned the cobwebs off the inside of this room.

"Sit down, sit down," Aunty Pauline said. She motioned to the couches then disappeared around the corner. She returned a moment later with a large, yellowed envelope.

"Since I returned from England last month, I've started sorting trunks and closets." She clapped her hands on her cheeks. "Oh, my. It's too much. I don't know why I thought I needed to come back after all these years and sell the house. I didn't need the money *that* badly. I must have had *a few kangaroos loose in the top paddock.*"

Chloe leaned over to Wendy and whispered, "She means she must have been foolish."

Aunty Pauline wagged her finger at Chloe. "More like crazy. I should have just stayed in England. Or I should have sold the house years ago along with everything in it. But then I wouldn't have found this." She shook the envelope in her hand. Something loose thudded inside. "This is for you." She handed the envelope to Jacko.

Jacko looked at his mom. She nodded slightly. He took the envelope and looked up at his great aunty. "But I can't read," he said solemnly. "I'm just starting *kindy*."

The old lady waved her hand like it didn't matter. "The man who wrote the letter has been dead for well over a hundred years. I don't think he cared if you could read."

"I'll help you, Jacko," Wendy said. She took the old envelope. The paper felt thick and brittle, like it would break if she bent it. It wasn't sealed like a normal envelope. Instead, it had a dried-out leather string tied around it. Big, flowery letters spread across the front.

Wendy studied the letters a moment and then figured it out. "It says, 'Jack.'" She looked up. The hair on the back of her neck stood up.

"Wait a minute!" Jacko said. His voice quivered. "This has my name on it? How does he know my name?"

Mrs. Taylor cleared her throat. "That was a common name then like it is now," she said, but she sounded nervous. "It's just a coincidence."

"Or maybe not," Aunty Pauline huffed.

"What do you mean?" Chloe asked. "What's a coincidence? Or maybe not?"

"Maybe it's part of the family curse," the old woman said. She raised an eyebrow.

"What?" Chloe asked nervously. "There's a

curse on our family? What do you mean?"

"There's not a curse on the family," Mrs. Taylor said sharply.

"There is, and you'd better tell your kids about it," the old lady argued and shook her finger at Mrs. Taylor. "My aunty warned your mum—"

"And my mum didn't believe it then either," Mrs. Taylor said.

"What's going on?" Chloe asked.

Mrs. Taylor didn't say anything. She just looked down at her hands.

"Laura, if you don't tell them, I will," the old lady said. "They have a right to know." She pointed at Jacko with her chin. "Especially the boy."

Mrs. Taylor stiffened. She locked her jaw.

Aunty Pauline looked at Chloe's mom and harrumphed. "So you didn't tell the boy?"

Mrs. Taylor's eyes darted from Jacko to Chloe and back to Jacko again. "No," she said firmly. "I don't believe the family is cursed. I didn't think it was important to tell them."

"Well," the old lady said and crossed her arms. "It's your birthday the day after tomorrow, boy?"

Jacko nodded. His eyes were huge.

"I guess we'll find out if the curse is true."

"No!" Mrs. Taylor said. Wendy had never heard her sound angry like this. "I'm sorry we came. I'm sorry my kids had to listen to this foolishness." She stood up. "Let's go!"

"Mum!" Chloe huffed. "Whatever it is, we need to know."

But Mrs. Taylor had already taken Jacko's hand and was pulling him toward the door.

Chloe stood but didn't move. She put her hands on her hips. "Mum, what's this about? You have to tell us."

Mrs. Taylor stopped and turned. Her shoulders drooped. She looked tired. "It's a silly family story, and it's made us afraid for no good reason."

Chloe looked at her great aunty. "What's the story?"

The old woman raised her eyebrows. She pulled a lacy handkerchief from her pocket and dabbed her forehead. "Laura?"

The old lady pointed to the yellowed envelope in Wendy's hands. "A long time ago, when this man was alive, he married a very bad woman. I don't know what happened, but ever

16

since, every boy in the family has had a serious accident before he turns six."

"Six?" Jacko nearly shouted. "My birthday is in two days. Does that mean—"

"No!" Mrs. Taylor said forcefully. "No. It's not true. You'll be fine." She pulled him close and hugged him. "They were accidents. Some farm accidents. One fell out of a tree. One ran out into traffic."

"All just before they turned six," Aunty Pauline added.

Wendy's heart pounded. She definitely should have stayed in the car. She bit her thumbnail.

The old lady tilted her chin at Wendy. "Read the letter."

Wendy looked at Mrs. Taylor, who slowly nodded her head. She'd clearly given up. Jacko slipped out of his mum's arms and plopped down on the couch beside Wendy.

Wendy carefully untied the dried-out leather string and opened the flap. The stiff envelope crackled slightly. She pulled out a single sheet of folded paper. But the envelope still had more in it. Wendy turned it upside down. Out dropped a rusty skeleton key.

Chapter 3

The Letter

Jacko picked up the key. "What's this for?"

"I think we'll have to read the letter to find out," Chloe said. She poked Wendy to begin.

Wendy unfolded the ancient, brittle paper. The same flowery letters covered the page. She examined the fancy writing. It would have been easier for her to read Chinese characters. She furrowed her brow and followed the lines the letters made. She could do this, but it would take some time.

"Dear Jack," she began. "It's with a heavy heart that I write this letter. I know that I'll soon be *pushing up daisies*."

Wendy looked up from the letter. "What does that mean? I just don't get what this is about."

"It means he's—" Chloe paused and looked at her mom, who nodded slightly. "It means he's dying." She whispered to Wendy, "This is creepy."

Wendy took a deep breath. Her hands shook slightly, but she began to read again. "This influenza will be the end of me. The doc says I might last the week or meet my maker tonight. Jack, it's important that I leave you some instructions. First of all, I hope you can forgive me for leaving you with your stepmum. I have few regrets from my life, but marrying Elsie is the biggest regret I have. Sadly, I worry that this one tragic mistake will tarnish all the many good things I have done. Elsie is very angry with me because I've stopped giving her money. So she says she's put a curse on our family. She says the curse will bring harm to our family for many generations."

"See?" Aunty Pauline interrupted and shook her finger at Mrs. Taylor. "I told you so."

"There's no such thing as a family curse," Mrs. Taylor argued back. "The trouble is, if you think there's a curse on you, then you think everything bad that happens is because of the curse." She softened her voice. "Keep reading, Wendy."

"Please understand how sad and lonely I was when your mum died. I was left with your sister, Mary, who was only four, and you. You were just days old. I feared I would have to put you in an orphanage. I had no way to care for you. And then Elsie showed up on my doorstep. She'd heard about your mum. She came with a pot of stew and to lend an extra hand. Her kindness in that moment overwhelmed me. I thought I loved her. But I know

now that I confused relief for love."

Wendy wished this would be a different kind of letter. It reminded her of losing her own father before she really knew him. It reminded her of how sad she felt sometimes because she didn't have a dad. She glanced at Chloe and Jacko. She wondered if they remembered she had no father.

"Keep reading," Jacko said. "What happens next?"

Wendy began again. "I know now that your stepmum never loved me either. She took advantage of us and our situation. She pretended to be kind to you and Mary, but she had a mean heart. She thought I had a lot of money, and she began to spend it on things for herself, never for you and Mary. And now the money is almost gone. I fear for the coming days and weeks. I fear even more for the coming years. Jack, you will be six in a few days—"

Jacko shuddered. "Why is it so much like me?"

"He's not like you," Mrs. Taylor said sharply. "You share the same name. And we just happen to be here at the same age he was. It's just a coincidence." She twisted a loose hair.

Wendy looked at Chloe. Chloe didn't look convinced. Wendy wasn't either. She began again. "Jack, you will be six in a few days. You must go to school this year. It's very important that you stay in school and learn to read and write. Elsie will try to make you work instead of going to school."

Jacko gasped. "*Hooly-dooly*! Work instead of going to *kindy*? That's nuts!"

Chloe shook her head. "What could a boy your age even do to make money?"

"Maybe sell newspapers or firewood," Mrs. Taylor said. "It wasn't all that unusual a hundred years ago. Children from poor families often had to work instead of going to school. Is there more to the letter, Wendy?"

Wendy nodded and continued. "If one of you must drop out of school to work, it should be your sister."

"What?" Now it was Chloe's turn to be mad. "She couldn't have been more than year four or five. Why should she have to drop out of school?"

Mrs. Taylor shook her head. "No one thought girls needed much of an education back then. Maybe he says more in the letter about why."

Wendy shook her head. She'd read a few more sentences to herself. "He just says what you said, Mrs. Taylor. 'A girl doesn't need that much education. She already has more than enough for being a cleaning girl or working in a store.'"

Chloe huffed. "As if that's all a girl would want to do." She crossed her arms.

Wendy continued reading, "Jack, you *must* stay in school. If you don't, you could end up a criminal like me."

"What?" all three kids shouted at the same time.

Mrs. Taylor looked at her aunty, who frowned. "It's true," Mrs. Taylor said and nodded her head.

"Why didn't you tell us this before?" Chloe asked.

"It's a long, complicated story. There never seemed a right time to talk about it," Mrs. Taylor said. "But now I guess we will."

Aunty Pauline huffed slightly.

Mrs. Taylor continued anyway. "He was born in England, but his father died when he was very young. He couldn't go to school but had to work to bring in a little money to buy food for the family.

One day when he was nine years old, he was so hungry he stole some beans."

"Beans?" Jacko asked.

"Beans," Mrs. Taylor said. "He was sentenced to seven years in prison."

Chloe gasped. "For stealing beans? That's unbelievable! Who would be so awful to do that?"

"Well that's a good question, and I don't have the answer. But it's a common story. Over 160,000 people came to Australia like your great-great-great-grandfather. As criminals," Mrs. Taylor said. "Back then, the British used Australia as a penal colony. That's like a jail. The British put your great-great-great-grandfather on a ship to Australia. He finished his sentence here, but he was never able to return to England. He never saw his mother or sisters and brothers again."

"You mean when he was nine he was sent away forever for stealing some beans?" Wendy asked.

"Chloe and I are nine." The girls looked at each other, their eyes wide.

"That's horrible!" Chloe said.

"Very!" Mrs. Taylor said. "The family story is that those early years were really tough. But he was hardworking. He eventually owned a store. In the end, he had some money. He died when the influenza plague hit Australia in 1900. That's about all I ever really knew. In fact, this letter tells us more than I knew about his life."

"There's a bit more to the letter," Wendy said. "Are you ready for me to finish?"

They all nodded.

"Safeguard this key. It's your only hope. Take it to the store and give it to Frank McGroody. He'll unlock the box I've saved for you. Inside the box, I have more instructions. It will explain how to end Elsie's curse on our family. Promise me, son, that you will study hard and that you will take care of your sister." Wendy looked up from the page. "It's signed, 'Your loving father.'"

"That's it? But what happened?" Chloe asked. "Did Jack read it? Did our great-great-great-grandfather die then? Why was the letter still in the envelope? How did you end up with the letter Aunty Pauline?"

"And why," Wendy added as she held up the rusty skeleton key, "was this still in the envelope?"

Chapter 4

The Old Trunk

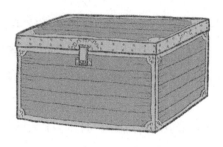

Aunty Pauline rubbed her chin. "I don't know. We know some things about your great-great-great-grandfather, but we don't know anything about Jack. We don't even know that much about his sister, Mary, who was my grandmother."

"Why don't you know more about them?" Wendy asked. She thought about the many stories she'd heard from her *lao lao* and *lao ye* about their parents and grandparents before they left China.

Aunty Pauline looked at Mrs. Taylor who looked at Chloe who looked at Wendy who looked at Jacko.

The gray-haired lady shuffled her feet a bit and studied her hands. Finally, she looked at Wendy and said, "I guess we just didn't talk about those things because there were so many sad events that had happened."

Wendy understood that. It had taken years for her own mom to talk about Wendy's dad's accident. "This all happened so long ago," she said. "Where can we find out more now?"

Aunty Pauline paused for a moment. "Well, I don't actually know. Maybe the cemetery would be the place to start. We'd at least find out when they died."

Wendy's neck tingled. This was definitely *not* what she thought she'd be doing in Sydney.

"Where is the cemetery?" Mrs. Taylor asked.

Wendy, Jacko, and Chloe all squeezed hands a tiny bit harder.

"Well, the cemetery that Henry Beck—your great-great-great-grandfather—is buried in is just up the street and around the corner." The old lady jerked her head in the direction of the cemetery. "It's less than a *k* away." She looked at Wendy. "A kilometer."

The five of them sat. They didn't talk. Wendy chewed on her fingernail. Mrs. Taylor twisted a loose strand of hair. Aunty Pauline furrowed her eyebrows. Chloe rested her chin on her hands. Wendy finally said, "Maybe there's another place to start looking." She *really* didn't want to go searching in a cemetery. "The letter said something about a store. Do you know what the name could be or where it was?" They all turned to Aunty Pauline again.

She scratched her head. "I don't remember any

details about the store. My grandmother would've been Jack's sister. She died when I was five." Aunty Pauline drummed her fingers on the arm of her chair. "I kind of remember her, but she certainly never talked about that part of her life."

"Wait a minute," Chloe said. She held up her hands like she was stopping traffic. "I'm confused. How can Jack's sister be your grandmother when the man who wrote this letter is our great-great-great-grandfather?"

Jacko nodded. "I don't get it. There are just way too many 'greats' that we're talking about."

Mrs. Taylor laughed. "I can see why. I can get a little confused myself." She searched her purse for a piece of paper and a pen. "Let me see if I can draw our family tree. I'll only put the names in that are important."

At the top of the paper she wrote Henry Beck. "This is the man who wrote the letter to his son, Jack." Underneath she wrote Mary and Jack. "These were his two children. We still don't know what happened to Jack. But we do know a bit about his sister, Mary." Below Mary's name she wrote two more names: Margaret and Jane. "Jane is my grandmother and Aunty Pauline's mum. Margaret is the great-aunty that my mum and I visited thirty years ago." She tilted her head toward Aunty Pauline. "You lived with Great-Aunty Margaret at the time."

Aunty Pauline nodded. "She never married and never had children. I never married and I didn't have children either. As she got older, everyone expected me to move in and take care of her." She wrinkled her nose. "I spent the last few months of her life here with her. Then I moved to England, where I've been the last thirty years."

Under Jane, Mrs. Taylor wrote Pauline and Susan. "Susan is my mother and your grandmother.

My mom and Aunty Pauline were sisters." Under Susan, Mrs. Taylor wrote Laura, Kelly, and Claire. "This is me and my two sisters. Kelly and Claire aren't important in the story, but it should help you get some of the family connections straight."

Chloe seemed to get it. Wendy stayed a little confused. But that was okay.

Under her own name, Laura, Mrs. Taylor wrote Chloe and Jack. When it was all done, Mrs. Taylor took out a red pen and drew a line from Chloe

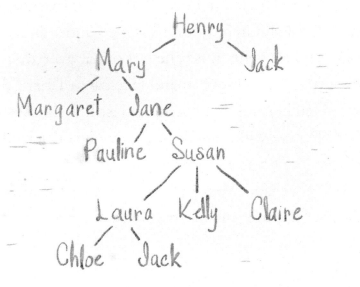

and Jack to Henry Beck. "So this is you. Me. Your grandma Susan. Your great-grandma Jane. Your great-great-grandma Mary. And your great-great-great-grandpa Henry."

"That helps," Chloe said. "Maybe we should just call them by their first names and not add all the 'greats.'"

"That's a good plan," Mrs. Taylor said. "We don't know what happened to Jack or even much about his sister Mary. If we knew what happened to them, maybe we would have an idea of why the envelope was never opened."

"And where the box is that Henry left for Jack," Chloe added. "If there really is a family curse, maybe there will be something in the box."

Wendy said, "Maybe there's something in the old trunk. You know, the one that had the envelope for Jack."

Aunty Pauline nodded her head slowly.

"Maybe." She led them all through the kitchen and on to the back *verandah* where a little breeze and a little shade made the air a little cooler. An ancient black trunk with leather straps sat against the house. It looked twice as big as the biggest suitcase Wendy and her mom had brought from California when they moved to Australia. If it had been empty Wendy could have climbed inside and hidden.

"A neighbor boy helped me drag the trunk outside. If I would have had to sort it in the shed I would have melted." She pointed with her chin to a weathered gray building at the end of the *verandah*. The old shed leaned slightly toward the house.

Aunty Pauline disappeared into the kitchen and in a few minutes reappeared. This time, she had a pitcher of icy lemonade and a plate of snacks.

"Have a *VoVo*," Aunty Pauline said. She put down a plate of cookies with stripes of pink marshmallow fluff and raspberry jam. Coconut covered everything but the bright red stripe of jam down the middle. "They're my favorite kind of *biscuit*."

Mrs. Taylor picked one up. "I haven't had one of these in years," she said between bites.

"YUM! These are the best *biscuits*!" Jacko wolfed one down in three bites. Chloe rolled her eyes.

Aunty Pauline opened the trunk while they munched on the *biscuits* and sipped the lemonade. The trunk held neatly stacked bundles of yellowed papers.

Aunty Pauline, Mrs. Taylor, Chloe, and Wendy each gently lifted out several bundles and untied the leather strings. Jacko sat on his chair, drank lemonade, and ate *biscuits*.

The bundles seemed to be mostly letters and postcards from people they didn't know.

"Wow! People wrote to each other a lot back then," Chloe said.

"They didn't have telephones or email," Mrs. Taylor said. "That was their only way to stay in touch."

They dug out some more bundles.

"Hey! I think I found something," Wendy said. "It's a stack of receipts from a store, H. C. Beck's Grocer and Mercantile. And look. Here's one with a date of the third of January 1900."

"Does it have an address?" Mrs. Taylor asked.

"244 Church Street," Wendy said.

"Here's another stack that has dates from 1903," Chloe said. "So either Henry didn't die then or someone kept his store going."

They dug deeper into the trunk and sorted through more bundles.

"Here are some bundles from 1905," Aunty Pauline said. "I don't see receipts with a later date. But there could be more receipts in other trunks. I just haven't had time to go through everything."

"Do you think it's still in business?" Wendy asked.

"I don't think so. It's been over a hundred years," Mrs. Taylor said. "But we'll find out tomorrow."

"No," Chloe answered. "We'll go looking for it today. We only have one day before Jacko turns six. We have to find out how to end Elsie's curse now!"

Chapter 5

H. E. Beck Grocer and Mercantile

They piled into the Taylor's car and headed toward 244 Church Street. At first, Aunty Pauline grumbled. "We're going to the old part of Sydney. Everything has been torn down and rebuilt. There won't be any old store there."

Mrs. Taylor said, "Let's go anyway. You never know what might still be standing or what people might know."

Aunty Pauline started giving directions: "Turn

here. Go straight. Go left at the roundabout."

Wendy felt lost and dizzy. Chloe didn't look like she felt any better. Jacko fell asleep.

"How can he do that?" Wendy asked Chloe.

"He's five-years old." Chloe rolled her eyes. "He's *knackered.*"

"Huh?" Wendy said.

"Tired," Chloe said. "When he's *knackered*, he can nap standing up."

The sun slipped lower on the horizon. Around them, the street caught the colors of the sunset. Reds and oranges and yellows. And then the shadows grew.

They raced along highways and twisted and turned through ancient narrow streets. Some of the old streets had abandoned warehouses. Most had freshly painted buildings.

They passed a huge sports arena.

"Is that a soccer stadium?" Wendy asked.

"Cricket," Aunty Pauline said.

"Crickets?" Wendy asked. She pictured millions of crickets crawling inside the stadium. She shuddered.

"No, cricket," Chloe said. "The game. You play it with a bat and a ball, but not like the bat and ball in baseball." She lowered her voice. "Good thing Jacko's not awake. He's *mad about* cricket."

Wendy wrinkled her nose. "Why is he mad about a game? It's just a game, right?"

Chloe laughed. "I mean he loves it. He'd make us stop right now even if all he did was run through the parking lot."

As they crossed a long bridge, Wendy pointed to a giant white building that sat on a finger of land. It looked like seashells propped on seashells. "What's that?"

"It's the Sydney Opera House," Chloe said. "It's famous and it's really cool. Mum got tickets for us to see a play there on Jacko's birthday."

The girls made eye contact. Neither one said the scary thing: If Jacko has another birthday. Chloe took her sleeping brother's hand.

Finally, Mrs. Taylor said, "We're here. This is the neighborhood." She pulled the car over and parked.

"But where are we?" Chloe said.

"We're close to the address on the receipt," Mrs. Taylor said. "It may be over a block or two. But we're within walking distance."

They shook Jacko awake and climbed out of the car. The wide street spread out in front of them. People and cars buzzed around them. Sunset arrived with a final burst of color.

They walked two blocks and studied the street numbers. They walked two more blocks and studied more street numbers. When they arrived at 244 Church Street, they might as well have been on Mars. Instead of an old grocery store, an upscale dress shop filled the space. Two tall, thin women dressed in black stood behind a counter.

"This doesn't look like it was ever H. C. Beck's Grocer and Mercantile," Wendy said.

"This is where Henry had his store?" Chloe asked. "It looks like if the family had kept it, we'd be gazillionaires today."

"Well," Mrs. Taylor said, "we would've had a lot of ups and downs between then and now."

H. E. Beck Grocer and Mercantile

"This building looks fairly new," Aunty Pauline said. "I wonder what happened to the original building." She took a deep breath, straightened her shoulders, and marched into the store. The women at the counter looked puzzled. Aunty Pauline waved her arms a bit. The saleswomen shrugged their shoulders. Aunty Pauline waved her arms a bit more. The saleswomen shrugged their shoulders a bit more. Aunty Pauline left the store and joined the others on the sidewalk.

"They said the building is only ten years old," Aunty Pauline reported. "Before it was built, the lot sat empty for over 100 years."

"Does that mean that we have the wrong address?" Chloe asked.

"Or does it mean that something happened to the store?" Wendy asked.

Chloe sighed, "Or maybe we're just at a dead end."

Chapter 6

The Cemetery Visit

Wendy was the first to talk. "What I don't understand is why the first Jack didn't open the envelope. Why didn't he do something with the key?"

"Especially," Chloe added, "since the letter said the key would unlock the box. And the box would tell Jack how to end the curse."

The three children were tucked away in an upstairs bedroom. They were supposed to be sound asleep. But how could anyone sleep with a rusty key a few feet away in the pocket of Jacko's shorts? A rusty key that would unlock a box. A rusty key that would end a curse. A rusty key that could save Jacko from something awful.

"There's got to be a reason," Chloe said. "If we just knew what happened to him."

"Well. Eventually he died, right?" Wendy asked. "Maybe if we knew when that happened, we'd know more."

"Maybe," Chloe said.

"What did your Aunty Pauline say about the cemetery?" Wendy asked. "If he's buried there, we might learn something more."

"She said it was just up the street and around the corner," Chloe said. "Less than a *k* away."

"Well then," Jacko said and sighed.

"Well then," Chloe repeated. She sighed too.

"Well then," Wendy said. But she didn't sigh.

Instead, she gathered up every ounce of courage she had and a little bit more. She had no idea from whom she borrowed that extra courage. "I think we should go see who is in the cemetery." She said that but she didn't honest to goodness think that. She wanted someone—anyone—to say, "How about if we all go to the cemetery next week? Around lunchtime." But that didn't happen, even though surely all three of them were thinking the same thing.

Except maybe Jacko, who said, "That's a great idea."

Wendy's neck tingled again. Being brave had its drawbacks.

"So we'll go tomorrow," Wendy said.

"No," Chloe said. "We have to go tonight. Jacko turns six the day after tomorrow. We can't waste any time."

So the three of them crawled out of their beds

and pulled their clothes back on. They tiptoed out of their room, down the stairs, and out the front door.

"Let's get the *torches* out of the car," Chloe whispered when they reached the *footpath*.

"*Torches?*" Wendy gasped. Her mother would *not* be happy about the three of them marching down the streets of Sydney with flaming sticks.

"Yes, *torches.*" Chloe pulled three flashlights out of the backseat pocket. She handed one to Wendy, who breathed a sigh of relief. She wouldn't accidently light anything on fire with a flashlight.

"We have to be quiet!" Chloe whispered. "Mum will kill us if she knows we're sneaking out."

"Well I guess it's handy we're already going to the cemetery," Wendy whispered back.

Nobody laughed.

"Which way?" Jacko asked.

"Aunty Pauline tilted her head in this direction,"

Chloe said. She pointed up the street.

They trudged in silence. One block. Two blocks. Three blocks. A sign read Shady Rest Cemetery. It pointed to the right. They followed the sign.

"Smells like rain," Wendy said. "Think we should turn around?"

The three of them looked up. Dark clouds slipped past the moon.

"A little rain never hurt anyone," Chloe said. "We don't have any time to waste."

A block later, they reached a black wrought iron fence. Beyond it they could see rows and rows and rows of grave markers.

"This is it," Chloe said.

Wendy pointed ahead. "There's the gate." She studied the space inside the fence. The cemetery didn't look all that big, maybe the size of her school playground back in San Francisco. Maybe a little larger. It looked like it hadn't been mowed in awhile. Weeds and shadows of weeds grew up against most of the headstones. A thick grove of trees lined the edges on three sides.

To Wendy, it didn't look a lot different from the tidy cemeteries she'd seen in San Francisco. These headstones were in English, though. Most of the headstones in the San Francisco cemeteries she'd been to had been in Chinese. But then, her *lao lao*, *lao ye*, and her mom were all Chinese. It occurred to her for the first time that maybe she'd only gone to Chinese cemeteries in San Francisco. She wondered if her San Francisco friends would think the cemetery looked familiar.

Chloe opened the gate. It squeaked. Eerrrkkkk. The three of them glanced around to see if anyone had heard. They only saw dancing shadows and more dancing shadows. Wendy hoped they were bushes and trees and not ghosts. She didn't know if she could trust her legs to run.

In the distance, thunder rumbled. Eerrrkkkk. Chloe closed the gate behind them.

"Are we sure this is a good idea?" Wendy asked. All she could think was that she must be crazy. She must be crazier than crazy, whatever that was. What in the world was she doing in a cemetery AT NIGHT in a country thousands of miles away from home?

Chloe only said. "Jacko's birthday." She didn't have to say more.

Far away, lightning flickered. Thunder boomed through the clouds again. The rain smelled close. Any other time, Wendy would have loved the scent.

"What's the name we're looking for?" Chloe asked.

"Henry Beck, Jack Beck, Mary—" Wendy said and stopped. She realized she didn't know Mary's married name.

The Cemetery Visit

"Let's start with Henry. What year did he die?" Chloe asked.

"The letter was dated the sixth of January 1900," Wendy said. "We should start with that."

"This isn't a very big cemetery," Chloe said. "If he's here, we'll find him."

"We should spread out," Wendy said.

"But I can't read," Jacko said. His voice shook.

"She'll be right," Wendy said. "We can look together. I'll look for the names, and you look for the dates. Look for anything where the man died in 1900. That will look like this." She took a stick and wrote the date in the dirt.

They scattered over the rows like a small flock of birds.

Their flashlights flickered over each headstone. Gray stone after gray stone lined up. Some stood tall. Some lay nearly buried in the scraggly grass. They had to study each one to make sure they didn't miss the name or the date.

Wendy and Jacko finished one row and started on the next one. Some gravestones had weathered so much they could hardly read the words, even with the light from their flashlights. Some had fancy writing that made it hard to figure out the person's name. Lots had Bible verses or bits of wisdom. None of them, though, had Henry Beck's name or death date. Wendy wondered if Aunty Pauline had been right. Was this the cemetery they were all buried in?

And then Chloe whooped from the far end of the row. "I found it! It's here!"

Wendy and Jacko raced to her.

"Look!" Chloe said and read the tombstone.

"Henry Beck Born Liverpool, England, 6 June 1854. Died 9 January 1900."

"And here's his first wife: Alice Beck. She died the thirteenth of January 1894," Wendy said. "That would have been about the time that Jack was born, right?"

Chloe nodded. "Mum was right. She must have died giving birth to Jack. I think that happened a lot back then." She shined the flashlight lower on the stone. "Oh, how sad. It says, 'A beautiful life cut short.'"

"And look," Wendy added. "Here's the stepmother, Elsie Beck. She died the ninth of April 1905." She held her flashlight steady on the small, flat grave marker.

"What's it say?" Jacko asked. He traced his finger over the words under Elsie's name.

Chloe read the inscription. "Mean and greedy till her last breath."

"Whoa! How awful!" Wendy said. "No wonder Mary didn't ever tell your aunty Pauline about her childhood. She would have lost her mom when she was four and then her father at ten."

"And then she lived with a horrible stepmum and became an orphan at fifteen," Chloe said. "What a tragic life."

They stared at the tombstones around them. Each one had a sad, sad story to tell. A fat drop of rain splattered on Wendy's forehead.

"Wait! Look at this!" Chloe said. "What was the name of the man Jack was supposed to give the key to?"

"Frank something," Wendy said. "Frank McGregor? Frank McGreevy?"

"Frank McGroody." Chloe shined her flashlight on a small headstone behind Henry Beck's. "And now we know why the key was still in the envelope. He died a week after Henry. He's buried here. He must have died from influenza too."

Thunder crashed overhead and the three of them jumped and screamed.

"Let's get out of here," Jack said. He twisted and began to run, then tripped over a flat marble grave marker next to Henry's. It was so white, it almost glowed in the dark. "Owwww!" he yelped and grabbed his shin.

Chloe bent down to look at his bloody leg. "Mum's going to kill us! We have to get back to the house."

"Wait!" Wendy said. "Take a look at this headstone." She rubbed her hand over the weathered stone. Her flashlight lit up the surface. "It says Jack Beck." She looked up at the other two. "It says 1900 just like the other one."

Chloe twisted around and studied the stone. "Not just 1900. It says 12 January 1900. He must have also died from influenza just three days after

his father." She shook her head. "Maybe he never even learned he had an envelope to open."

"Oh my," Wendy gasped. "Look at the dates. Born 13 January 1894. Died 12 January 1900." She stared at Jacko. "He died the day before his sixth birthday."

"Hooly-dooly!" Jacko and Chloe said together.

Lightning zagged into the trees behind them at the same time thunder boomed only feet away. The headstones seemed to crackle to life around them. Shadows danced on every grave. The skies opened and raindrops flew fast and furiously.

In unison, they shouted, "Run!"

Chapter 7

The Brilliant Idea

The sun rose too early. At 5:47 a.m. when the sun peaked over the horizon, Jacko's eyes were at the wrong place at the wrong time. And if he couldn't sleep, no one else could either.

"Chloe. Wendy." He gently shook them both. "Are you awake?"

"We are now, Jacko," Chloe groaned. She rolled over and closed her eyes again.

"Chloe, wake up! We have to find the box

and stop the curse before—" Jacko's voice caught. "Before tomorrow."

The girls crawled out of bed and they all headed downstairs. Mrs. Taylor and Aunty Pauline already sat on the *verandah* drinking tea.

"Jacko! What happened to your shin?" Mrs. Taylor asked.

They all looked down at Jacko's leg. The cut from his fall had dried blood around it and a big purple bruise.

"I fell in the cemetery last night," Jacko said. He gingerly felt around the cut.

Chloe rolled her eyes at Wendy and shook her head.

"You what? Where?" Mrs. Taylor put her fist on her hip. She looked at Chloe and wagged her finger. "You snuck out—"

Aunty Pauline burst out laughing. "You snuck out of the house and went to the cemetery after dark? You are three brave kids. I'd be too scared to do that. And in that thunderstorm?" When she caught her breath, she added, "Laura, you're raising these kids right." She chuckled some more and wiped the tears from her eyes.

Mrs. Taylor gritted her teeth. Her fist stayed on her hip, but her other hand stopped the finger wagging. "I can't believe you did that. And don't do it again!" She pointed straight at Chloe. Mrs. Taylor was not happy.

"Yes, Mum," Chloe said. "You won't believe what we found out though." She ran through the list of headstones they'd discovered, finishing with Jack Beck's.

"That explains a lot. But it's still not okay that you snuck out last night," Mrs. Taylor said. "You and I will have a conversation about this later."

Chloe sighed and nodded her head.

Mrs. Taylor continued, "I wonder what it means that Elsie died in 1905 and the receipts from the store end in 1905. Do you remember the date of her death?"

"April ninth," Wendy said.

"Let's look at those receipts again and see what the last dates are," Chloe said. "Maybe that will give us a clue."

They clustered around the trunk once again. This time they looked for the newest receipt.

"I don't see anything newer than 1905," Chloe

said. "Aunty Pauline, you're looking at the stack from 1905. What are you finding?"

"This is interesting. The receipts are here from January, February, and March. But the only receipts for April are for the ninth." She looked up. "The day Elsie died. What could that mean?"

"Do you have a public library in Sydney?" Wendy asked.

"Of course, dear," Aunty Pauline said. "Why do you ask?"

"In the main library in San Francisco, they have copies of all the old newspapers. If the Sydney library has old newspapers, maybe there will be a newspaper article that tells us something."

"That's brilliant, Wendy," Mrs. Taylor said. "How did you think of that?"

Wendy smiled sadly. "My dad died in an accident when I was two. When I was eight, my mom took me to the library. Together we looked up the article about my dad's accident. It helped to see it in the newspaper like that." She remembered that she and her mom went for ice cream afterwards.

"That's very sad about your dad. I can imagine it would have helped to see the newspaper article," Mrs. Taylor said.

Wendy nodded but didn't say anything.

"Can we go to the library?" Jacko asked.

"Absolutely," Mrs. Taylor said. "I want to pick up the tickets for the play tomorrow and run some errands. I'll drop you off at the library on the way and pick you up when I'm done."

Chloe began, "What if they don't have—"

Wendy stopped her. "Don't say that. We're going to find something important." She took a deep breath. "We just have to."

Chapter 8

The Discovery

A few short hours later, Wendy, Chloe, and Jacko climbed up the few short steps to the Customs House Library. Wendy loved the simple, clean lines of the building. Two balconies stretched across the middle of the four-story white stone building. A giant clock above the balconies gonged the hour. She wondered what it must have been like a hundred years earlier when it was a true customs house. It would have been the first stopping point in the country for many people.

They found the front desk and asked about where to find old newspapers. The receptionist pulled out a map. She drew arrows to take them to the right spot.

They wound their way up the stairs and into a room with tall windows and massive dark wood tables. An elderly woman sat at a tidy desk at the entrance. A halo of curly red hair circled her face. Thin reading glasses perched on the very end of her nose. If she sneezed, they would have landed across the room.

Chloe spoke first. "We're looking for a newspaper from the ninth of April 1905. Can you show us how to find one?"

The librarian tipped her nose down and looked over her glasses. "Do you have your library card?"

Chloe's, Jacko's, and Wendy's eyes shifted left then right then left again.

"Our aunty has it," Chloe said. She sounded very formal.

"Well, where is she?" the librarian asked.

There was a long pause and more eye shifting. "In the *loo*," Chloe finally said. Her head bobbed up and down. "In the *loo*," she said again.

The librarian looked at her computer. Wendy turned to Chloe and mouthed, "In the bathroom? What?"

Chloe gave her a helpless shrug and mouthed back. "She could be."

"We can wait," the librarian said.

Jacko looked up at his sister. His eyes grew big. "It could be awhile before she gets here," he said.

"We don't know *what* she had for *brekkie*," Wendy said. At least that part was true.

"Oh, poor thing," the librarian said. "Well let's just see what we can find."

She led them over to file drawers and pulled out

a white square box. She emptied a wide film spool. Then she threaded the film through a complicated looking machine. "This is *The Sydney Morning Herald*. It's been around almost 200 years. If there was any news on the ninth of April 1905, it'll have it." She spent a couple minutes showing them how to move the film. And then she sped it up to April nine. "Here's the date you're looking for."

"There aren't very many pictures," Jacko said.

"No," the librarian said. "It was different then. They had to take the picture and develop it. So it wasn't fast. It had to be something major to have a photograph. It's not like now. Papers today use a lot of photos because it's all digital."

They studied the front page. Nothing jumped out.

"Do you see what you're looking for?" the librarian asked. "It could have been on one of the later pages."

"We're looking for a woman who died April ninth," Wendy said. "Other than that, we don't know exactly what we're looking for."

"Oh. Well, her obituary wouldn't have been on the day she died," the librarian said. "It could be up to a week later. It depended on the family."

She scrolled on to April ten and to the obituary page. "Recognize any names?"

They skimmed the page and shook their heads. She moved on to the eleventh and then the twelfth. "Now do you see anything?"

"There," Chloe said and pointed to the spot on the page. "Elsie Beck."

The print was fuzzy, but they could still make it out.

"Elsie Beck, wife of the late Henry

The Discovery

E. Beck, passed away 9 April when she was struck by a horse and carriage as she fled the fire that consumed H.E. Beck Grocer and Mercantile. She was preceded in death by a stepson, Jack Beck. She leaves behind a stepdaughter, Mary Beck."

"Well, that was short and sweet," the librarian said. She looked a little confused. "Often the obituaries go on and on. Just look at the others on the page."

"Can we print this page?" Wendy asked.

"Sure. Just press this button." The librarian pressed it for them. "If you print more than ten pages you have to pay." The printer started humming. "Need anything else?"

"Maybe we'll look to see if there was anything about the fire in an earlier paper," Chloe said.

"Sure thing. I need to get back to my desk, but if you need anything else, let me know." She turned and left.

"Here's what I think," Wendy said. "If the fire was on the ninth, it wouldn't have made the paper until the tenth. Or even the eleventh. Let's scroll back."

They scrolled back to April ten and studied the articles on the front page.

"Here it is," Wendy said. She read the important bits out loud for Jacko. "A fire demolished the H. E Beck Grocer and Mercantile establishment on the evening of 9 April. The cause is unknown at this time. Elsie Beck, owner and widow of H. E. Beck, fled the building as the flames grew. She carried a wooden box—"

Jacko shrieked, "She had the box! She had the box!"

"Shhhhh!" the girls both said. They glanced around. The librarian frowned in their direction.

Wendy's heart pounded. "We don't know if it's *the* box. It might have been the money box. Or the receipt box." But she hoped, hoped, hoped it was *the* box.

She kept reading. "She carried a wooden box with her as she fled into the street. Sadly, she dropped the box. When she bent to pick it up, she was hit by a passing horse and carriage. She died before she reached the hospital. Her stepdaughter, Mary Beck, escaped the flames. Friends have taken her in as she recovers. The store burned to ashes in spite of the fire brigade's heroic efforts to put out the blaze."

"I feel jittery," Chloe said.

"Me too," Wendy said. "We're close." She pressed the print button. Pages spit out of the printer.

"Yes," Chloe said. "But we still have no idea where the box ended up."

"What do we do now?" Jacko asked.

"I don't know," Chloe said. "I just don't know."

Chapter 9

The Box

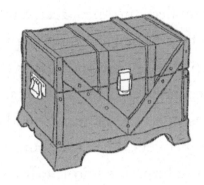

The three kids sat on the steps of the library and waited for Mrs. Taylor. They sat with their chins on their hands and their elbows on their knees. The sun beat down on them. Sweat trickled down their necks. Wendy felt like she was in a sauna.

"We know the box survived the fire," Chloe said.

"No. We know *a* box survived the fire," Wendy said. "And even if it was *the* box, we don't know if anything was still inside it. Besides, for all we know, it might have been the cash or receipt box."

"I don't think it was the receipt box. If it had been, we would have found all the April receipts in the trunk. But we only found the receipts for one day," Chloe pointed out.

"True," Wendy said. She thought for a minute. "I bet Elsie grabbed the receipts and the money from that day."

Chloe snapped her fingers. "What did Elsie's tombstone say?"

"Mean and greedy to her last breath," Wendy said.

Chloe asked, "Was she so greedy over a few dollars from that day that she would've risked her life to pick up the box?" She answered her own question. "Maybe. But I think it was far more valuable than that. It had to be whatever Henry Beck tried to leave his son."

"The box is at your aunty Pauline's," Wendy said.

"How do you know?" Chloe asked.

Wendy responded, "It has to be. It might be empty, but the box didn't just get left in the street."

"Mum!" Jacko called out and waved.

Mrs. Taylor pulled over and the three kids jumped in. "Did you find out anything?" She asked once they were on the road again.

Chloe waved the papers from the library at Mrs. Taylor. "We found out everything. Except what was in the box."

"And if whatever was in the box *then* is still in the box *now*," Wendy added.

"So you know where the box is?" Mrs. Taylor asked. Wendy could hear the excitement in her voice.

All three kids sighed at the same time. "No."

"But we think it might be back at Aunty Pauline's," Jacko said.

"We don't know where else to look for it," Chloe said. "She said herself that the shed was full of all kinds of trunks and boxes that she hadn't gone through. Maybe it's buried in there."

"Then that's our next step," Mrs. Taylor said.

Aunty Pauline had a late lunch of meat pies made of finely chopped beef, onions, and tomato sauce ready for them. For dessert, she'd fixed colorfully layered fruit in glasses—blueberries, strawberries, mangos, bananas, and grapes. Wendy took a photo of it with her mom's old phone so she'd remember to tell her mom about it. They ate on the back *verandah* while the kids filled in the details of what they'd learned. Mrs. Taylor looked at Wendy. "I'll say it again. Your idea of going to the library was brilliant."

Wendy blushed. The compliment felt nice.

"Well," Aunty Pauline said. She blew some loose curls off her forehead. "I don't know where we start to look. Aunty Margaret must have kept every single thing she ever owned. That includes all the things my grandma Mary kept. You should see that shed."

Chloe and Wendy looked at each other. "If

they kept everything she ever owned," Wendy said, "surely they must have kept the box. Even if it's empty, we want to find it."

"We can start looking later this *arvo*—this afternoon. It'll be cooler in the shed then," Aunty Pauline said.

Chloe shook her head. "No. Jacko's birthday is tomorrow. We should start right now."

Aunty Pauline sighed. But she gathered up the lunch dishes and carried them inside. "Follow me," she said.

The four of them followed her back outside. They headed to the end of the *verandah* to the leaning shed.

Aunty Pauline grumbled. "I have to warn you. It's hot and dusty in there." She brushed a damp curl of hair off her neck and unlocked the door.

The kids got the first peek.

"*Hooly-dooly*! This is like hunting for lost

The Box

treasure," Jacko exclaimed. "Look at all these boxes and trunks!"

Wendy wilted. Aunty Pauline had been right. The place was packed. It could take ten years to find anything.

"Where do we start?" Mrs. Taylor said. Wendy thought she looked wilted, too.

"The trunk with Jack's letter was in that corner." She pointed to a space by a tiny window. "I've already sorted through those boxes behind it. Most of it will go to charity. There's not much worth saving."

"Then that's a good place for us to start," Mrs. Taylor said.

"What sized box are we looking for?" Chloe asked.

They all looked at each other. "Who knows?" Mrs. Taylor said. "There wasn't a description in Henry's letter."

The Box

"Watch out for spiders," Aunty Pauline cautioned. "I think I've chased all the snakes out of here already." She muttered something under her breath.

Wendy shuddered. She looked at Chloe who just shrugged her shoulders. "It's Australia," she said. "We have 2,400 spider species. But don't worry. Only about fifty of them are poisonous."

"*Hooly-dooly*!" Wendy exclaimed. "And that's supposed to make me feel better?"

Mrs. Taylor just laughed. "Well, I've survived this long. I'm sure you'll make it through the afternoon."

They each took a box and started the hunt. (Wendy started her hunt very, very, very carefully!) Some boxes held old clothes or blankets. Others had hats, gloves, and purses. Still others had worn out shoes. Some had books with faded covers. A few had papers neatly stacked inside. Most, though, were filled with odds and ends—candleholders, dishes, broken toys, yellowed doilies, or old toiletries.

Every now and then one of them would pull out something interesting: shoes with bowties or hats with colorful feathers or a furry purse with rabbit paws. "Look at this!" The rest would laugh at how funny or pretty or weird it looked and then keep on sorting. Even Jacko stuck with it.

They worked through the afternoon and well into the evening. They took time to cool off with ginger ale and scones with jam and cream on the *verandah* and, in Aunty Pauline's case because she was *knackered*, a late-afternoon nap.

By the time they stopped for a super late dinner, they'd given a quick look to maybe a quarter of the boxes and trunks. Nothing seemed even close to holding a box so important.

They ordered fish and chips for—as Chloe called it—*takeaway* and sat on the back *verandah* again. The air had cooled slightly from the day. In the distance, a flash of lightning lit up the horizon.

The Box

"Think it'll rain again?" Mrs. Taylor asked.

"It might," Aunty Pauline said. "This is the season for stormy weather."

They munched on the fish and chips and drank their lemonade. Thunder rumbled far away. The kids should have been sound asleep by now, but all three wanted to keep searching through the shed. "I can stay up all night if I have to," Jacko said. But then he yawned, which made everyone laugh.

All of a sudden, Chloe said, "Wait a minute. We're thinking about this backwards."

"What do you mean?" Mrs. Taylor asked.

"Wendy." She turned to her friend. "What's the most important thing you brought with you from San Francisco?"

Wendy didn't even have to think about that. "The photo of my grandparents, my *lao lao* and *lao ye*. I miss them every day."

"Exactly!" Chloe said. She grew excited. "And

where do you have that photo?"

"Right beside my bed. It's the last thing I see before I go to sleep and the first thing I see in the morning." Wendy cocked her head to the side. "But what does that have to do with the box?"

"Think about it," Chloe asked. "If that box was something from your father and that box saved you from a horrible stepmum, would you just pack it in a trunk and put it in a shed? I don't think so." She turned to her aunty Pauline. "Which room did your grandma Mary use as her bedroom?"

"The one above the living room. My aunty Margaret slept across the hall. That's the room I'm using now." She stopped and thought a minute. "My grandma's room was full of her special things and Aunty Margaret kept it that way. I was saving that for last to sort through because I knew there would be things to keep or sell, not just give away."

"That's it," Chloe said and put down her plate.

The Box

They all jumped up from the table. The kids raced up the stairs. Mrs. Taylor and even Aunty Pauline were only three steps behind.

Chloe threw open the bedroom door. Warm, musty air greeted them. Cobwebs stretched across the corners. A fine layer of dust covered everything. All eyes scanned the room: the bed stand, the dresser, and finally the shelf above the dresser. The shelf that was opposite of the bed. The shelf that would have been the last thing Mary saw before she

closed her eyes and the first thing she saw when she opened them.

Dead center on the shelf sat an ancient wooden box.

They all whooped and hugged each other.

"Chloe, that was brilliant!" Mrs. Taylor said and threw her arms around her. "I can't believe you thought of that!" She reached up and took the box down. "This has to be it." She gently shook it and looked at the others. There's something in it."

"Mum, there's a letter taped to the bottom," Jacko said.

Mrs. Taylor peeled off the letter and handed it to Chloe. "You read it. We never would've thought to look under our noses if you hadn't figured it out."

Chloe slit open the envelope with her finger and took out a single sheet of yellowed paper. She read, "This box saved my life. Elsie had spent all the money the store made, so the bank was taking the store from us. We had nothing left. On 9 April 1905, our last day there, I was cleaning a high shelf and found this box. Both Elsie and I knew there was something that father had put away for Jack before he died, but we'd never found it. We thought it was something very valuable. When she saw the box, we had a fight. She grabbed it out of my hands and then threw a gas lantern to the floor. She thought I would die in the fire. She ran out of the store. I dashed through the flames and followed her into the street. Elsie dropped the box and then a horse and carriage hit her. I saw Elsie take her last breath as I picked up the box. I do not have the key to open this, but I don't care. It saved me."

No one said a word. No one even breathed. The clock downstairs gonged eleven.

And then Jacko said, "Uh oh." He patted his pockets then pulled them inside out.

"What?" they all said.

"I lost the key."

"What?" they all said again.

"It's not in my pocket. It must have fallen out." He looked ready to cry.

Chloe put her arms around him. "We'll find it. Don't worry. When was the last time you know you had it?"

He thought a minute. He looked at Chloe and then Wendy. "Last night at the cemetery?"

"When you fell!" both girls said together.

"Let's go!" Wendy said and grabbed his hand.

"Now?" Mrs. Taylor said. "Wait for the storm to pass."

"No, Mum," Chloe said. "Jacko turns six tomorrow."

"But the curse isn't real," Mrs. Taylor pleaded.

"We're not taking a chance," Chloe said. She raced out the door, down the stairs, and out on the street just steps behind Wendy and Jacko.

Fat raindrops splattered the pavement.

The Box

Lightning flashed up ahead and seconds later thunder cracked.

"But what about the lightning?" Wendy shouted to Chloe and tilted her head toward Jacko.

"He's not going to get hurt!" Chloe shouted back. "We have to believe that!"

The three grabbed hands and ran all the way to the cemetery.

Eerrrkkkk. The gate squeaked open. The rain fell faster and harder. Again, the lightning flashed, this time closer. The sky rumbled above them only seconds later.

They stumbled through the rain to the grave of Jack Beck and dropped to their knees. Raindrops splashed around them, making a splat, splat, splat sound.

"It's here," Wendy said. "It's got to be here." She wiped the wet hair out of her eyes.

They clawed through the grass and patted the

dirt—now goopy mud—around Jack Beck's glowing white headstone. Nothing. No key.

"Keep looking," Chloe hollered over the storm. "We have to find it."

The three of them pawed through the grass. The rain dashed against the headstones around them.

Lightning flared and thunder crashed. In that brief second of light, Jacko saw the key. It had fallen in front of Henry Beck's gravestone. The key had come home.

Chapter 10

The Gift

Click.

It was the sweetest sound any of them could hope for. The box sprung open. Inside lay a single penny, a black velvet bag and a folded piece of paper.

Mrs. Taylor handed the paper to Chloe to read.

Dear Jack,

I am sad that you are reading this letter. It means I have not survived this plague of influenza. I have put coins in this box. It is the last of my money. You should be able to get most of what you need from our own store, H. C. Beck's Grocer and Mercantile, so you will not starve. The rest of the money should give you and Mary enough to buy a few clothes and shoes as you grow up and for other small necessities. But you must live simply. In eight or ten years, Mary will have a husband, and you will be educated enough to run the store. Until that day, Mr. McGroody will take care of the store. Give these coins to Mr. McGroody. You can trust him. He will pay your bills for you. When you take over the store, be sure to take care of Mr. McGroody. He is a good and honest man.

Whatever you do, do not give the money to Elsie. Your stepmum will want you to work instead of going to school. Do not do this. Study and make something of yourself.

Elsie will tell you she's cursed the family because I wouldn't give her money. Give her the penny in this box. Tell her that I am giving her everything I owe her. She will be very angry, but if I give her money—any money—she will have to admit that the curse is broken. She'll have gotten what she demanded—more money.

The truth is, though, no matter what Elsie says, there's no such thing as a curse. We choose our own paths. I know this is true. Look at my life that started in sadness and gave me two children who give me so much joy. Someone even as wicked as Elsie cannot ruin your life unless you let her. Make sure the path you choose is one that will make you happy. Make the most of every day.

I'm sorry to leave you at such a tender age. You and Mary have been a gift to me.

Your loving father

Chloe folded the paper and put it in the box. Everyone felt a little teary.

"Life was more difficult then," Mrs. Taylor said. She hugged both of her kids, and then she hugged Wendy.

"So there really wasn't a family curse?" Jacko asked.

"No." Mrs. Taylor looked at Aunty Pauline. "There never was. It was just chance that the other boys had those accidents."

"You're sure?" Jacko asked.

Mrs. Taylor smiled. "I'm positive," she said. "You're going to live a long, good life."

Chloe hugged her brother and handed him the black velvet bag. "I think you should do the honors."

Jacko took the bag and shook the coins into the box. He shouted, "Whoa! We're rich!"

Mrs. Taylor laughed. "We aren't rich. I don't even know what these coins are worth. I'm sure, though, that this will help with the sheep *station*. And remember, only half is ours. The other half is Aunty Pauline's."

Aunty Pauline harrumphed. "I'm fine. I'll take a few of these coins, but your family should have the rest. And Wendy and her mum should have a few.

The Gift

Without her, we never would have realized the box could be in this house." She scooted some coins across the table to Wendy.

On the floor below them, the clock gonged twelve. It was later than any of them should've been up.

"Whoohoo!" Chloe hugged her brother again. "See? There really is no curse!"

"Happy birthday, Jacko," Wendy said. "We're glad we're all here to celebrate it with you."

Sneak Peek of Another Adventure

Mystery of the Lazy Loggerhead

Chapter One

"What's that?" Sofia Diaz asked.

"Onde?" Her Brazilian friend, Júlia Santos, scanned the edge of the beach. She squinted from the early morning rays of the sun. "Where? I don't see anything?"

"It's moving." Sofia kicked her new Havaianas off her tan feet. She made sure to pick them up. They were only the most famous flip flops in the world. She did NOT want to lose them. Sandals safely in hand, she dashed down the beach. The familiar smell of the salt air filled her lungs. The sand kicked up behind her speedy feet.

Sofia stopped a few yards away and pointed. "It's a sea turtle. See her giant head and big jaws?

And the reddish-brown and yellow color of her shell? I think she's a loggerhead."

"How do you know she is, how do you say, logger—head?" Júlia asked.

"I know a little about sea turtles." Sofia said. "My grandparents in Florida live near a sea turtle rescue place. I've seen loads of loggerheads there. And she looks the same. She seems slow though."

"Turtles are *all* slow, no?" Júlia giggled. Her brown eyes sparkled. Her light brown skin glowed in the sun.

Sofia spun around and smiled. "Yesssss. But she seems really, really slow. I hope she's not sick."

Júlia shrugged her shoulders. "*Preguiçoso?* Maybe she is lazy?"

"Look!" Sofia pointed at the sand ahead.

Júlia stared at the strange markings in the sand. "They look like small tire tracks."

Sofia kneeled down to inspect the tracks. "They

are tracks. But not from tires. From a sea turtle."

"Do you think the lazy loggerhead made them?" Júlia scratched her head.

"Maybe." Sofia looked up and scanned the beach. The lazy loggerhead still crawled slowly along the water's edge.

Júlia knelt down and brushed her hand over the tracks. "Or do you think she led us here?"

"Well, normally, I would say no. But after the troubled toucan . . ." Sofia tilted her head to one side. "Never say never."

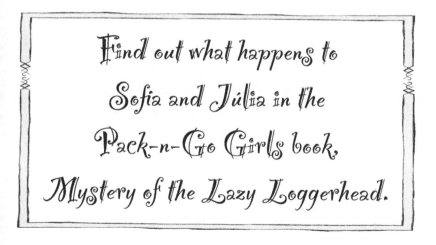

Find out what happens to Sofia and Júlia in the Pack-n-Go Girls book, Mystery of the Lazy Loggerhead.

Dive into More Reading Fun!

Discover Brazil with Sofia and Júlia!

Mystery of the Troubled Toucan

Nine-year-old Sofia Diaz's world is coming apart. So is the rickety old boat that carries her far up the Rio Negro river in Brazil. Crocodiles swim in the dark waters. Spiders scurry up the twisted tree trunks. And a crazy toucan screeches a warning. It chases Sofia and Júlia, her new friend, deep into the steamy rainforest. There they stumble upon a shocking discovery. Don't miss the second Brazil book, *Mystery of the Lazy Loggerhead.*

Discover Thailand with Jess and Nong May!

Mystery of the Golden Temple

Nong May and her family have had a lot of bad luck lately. When nine-year-old Jess arrives in Thailand and accidentally breaks a special family treasure, it seems to only get worse. It turns out the treasure holds a secret that could change things forever!

Meet More Pack-n-Go Girls!

Discover Mexico with Izzy and Patti!

Mystery of the Thief in the Night
Izzy's family sails into a quiet lagoon in Mexico and drops their anchor. Izzy can't wait to explore the pretty little village, eat yummy tacos, and practice her Spanish. When she meets nine-year-old Patti, Izzy's thrilled. Now she can do all that and have a new friend to play with too. Life is perfect. At least it's perfect until they realize there's a midnight thief on the loose! Don't miss the second Mexico book, *Mystery of the Disappearing Dolphin.*

Discover Austria with Brooke and Eva!

Mystery of the Ballerina Ghost
Nine-year-old Brooke Mason is headed to Austria. She'll stay in Schloss Mueller, an ancient Austrian castle. Eva, the girl who lives in Schloss Mueller, is thrilled to meet Brooke. Unfortunately, the castle's ghost isn't quite so happy. Don't miss the second and third Austria books: *Mystery of the Secret Room* and *Mystery at the Christmas Market.*

What to Know Before You Go!

Where is Australia?

Australia is both a country and a continent in the Southern Hemisphere. It's often called an island country because it's the only country on the continent. As a country, it includes the island of Tasmania and other small islands. It's the sixth largest country in the world in area and is completely surrounded by water. But it has only about 23,000,000 people, so it's fifty-fifth in population. The country has only six states. The outback, which is a desert, covers much of the country. Australia became a country in 1901.

Australian Money

Did you know that every country has its own money? In the United States, we use dollars and cents for our money system. Australia also uses dollars and cents, but they don't look the same as ours. The bills are pink, red, blue, yellow, and green, and they come in different sizes. They also have different denominations. You'll find $5, $10, $20, $50, and $100 bills. For coins, Australians use 5c, 10c, 20c, 50c, $1, and $2.

We use this symbol to mean dollar: $. The symbol for the Australian dollar is the same: $. If you go to Australia, you won't be able to use American dollars or change. Instead, your mom and dad can go to a bank to change their U.S. dollars for Australian dollars. Or they can use an ATM to get money from their bank account. The money that comes out of the bank machine will be Australian dollars, of course!

What to See in Sydney

Sydney is perhaps the best-known city in Australia. And the best-known site is the Sydney Opera House, which does in fact look like seashells propped on seashells. If you visit, make sure you check out their upcoming shows. Sydney is also well known for its beautiful beaches. If you want a little excitement, you can feed a fifteen-foot saltwater crocodile at the Wild Life Sydney Zoo. Or explore the Australian Reptile Park and Wildlife Sanctuary about an hour north of Sydney.

A Little Australian History

Australia was originally settled by Aboriginal people at least 50,000 years ago. Europeans arrived much more recently. A Dutch explorer landed in 1606. In 1770, the British claimed the continent as part of their territory. Within a few years, they started sending British prisoners to Australia. Between 1788 and 1868, they sent about 162,000 convicts to Australia. Some were sent for serious crimes, but many were like Henry Beck. They had the misfortune of just being poor and hungry. Their crimes were for stealing a few beans or a loaf of bread. About twenty percent of Australians today are descendants of early prisoners.

What Australians Eat

If you visit Australia, you'll find lots of familiar fruits: apples, pineapples, berries, grapes, and citrus. Since part of Australia is in the tropics, you'll also find plenty of less familiar tropical fruits, such as mangos, kiwi, passionfruit, jackfruit, papaya, starfruit, and others. Here's a fun and easy way to enjoy a taste of Australia for dinner tonight. The fruits in the recipe are a suggestion. Feel free to substitute whatever fruits you can find in your local store.

Aussie Fruit Salad

If you make this recipe, be sure you get an adult to help you peel and cut the fruit.

Ingredients:

- 3 kiwi, peeled and cubed
- 2 mangos, peeled and cubed
- 1 cup strawberries, sliced
- 1 cup blueberries
- 1 banana, sliced
- 5 teaspoons sugar

1. Mix each fruit separately with 1 teaspoon of sugar.
2. In four serving glasses, layer the fruit. For instance, layer strawberry, kiwi, banana, mango, and blueberry. Just for fun, you can layer each serving differently. Chill until you're ready to eat.

Say It in Australian!

Both Australians and Americans speak English. But the two countries pronounce words in different ways. Sometimes they have different meanings, too. For instance, we wear sweaters, but Australians wear jumpers. Australians also have lots of slang, or colorful ways, to describe things. You've already discovered some of this slang in *Mystery of the Min Min Lights* and *Mystery of the Rusty Key*. For more fun examples, check out the Pack-n-Go Girls website: www.packngogirls.com.

American English	Australian English
Hello	G'day
How's it going?	'Ow yar goin'?
My goodness!	Hooly dooly
Kindergarten	Kindy
Ranch or farm	Station
No worries	No drama
No worries	She'll be right
Porch	Verandah
Breakfast	Brekkie
Bathroom	Loo
Pasture	Paddock
Flashlight	Torch

American English	Australian English
Kilometer	K
Sidewalk	Footpath
Argument	Bit of a blue
Aunt	Aunty
Foolish or crazy	A few kangaroos loose in the top paddock
Passed away	Pushing up daisies
Cookie	Biscuit
Australian cookie	VoVo
Afternoon	Arvo
Mom	Mum
Tired	Knackered
Crazy about	Mad about
Carryout	Takeaway
Friend	Mate (boy) or Love (girl)
It's fine	She's apples

My Australian Trip Planner

Where to go: _____

_____

_____
_____
_____
_____
_____
_____
_____
_____
_____
_____
_____
_____
_____
_____

What to do: _____

_____

My ☑
Australian
Trip
Planner

_____

_____

_____

_____

_____

_____

_____

_____

_____

_____

_____

_____

_____

_____

_____

Things I want to pack:

_____

_____

_____

_____

_____

_____

_____

_____

_____

_____

_____

_____

_____

_____

_____

Friends to send postcards to:

My Australian Trip Planner

_____

_____

_____

_____

_____

_____

_____

_____

_____

_____

_____

_____

_____

Thank you to the following Pack-n-Go Girls:

Leee Bautista
Elizabeth De Pry
Havana Edwards
Lucia Ricotta
Sarah Travis

Thank you also to Rob Allan and his grammarian mother; Sarah Hudson, who was invaluable in her guidance regarding all things Aussie; Tina Troyer and Diana De Pry for their important suggestions and ongoing support; and Miriam D'Souza who triggered the original ideas and gave immense help in editing. Someday I'll make sure to spend a little time exploring haunted Sydney!

And a special thanks to my Pack-n-Go Girls co-founder, Lisa Travis, and our husbands, Steve Diller and Rich Travis, who have been along with us on this adventure.

Janelle Diller has always had a passion for writing. As a young child, she wouldn't leave home without a pad and pencil just in case her novel hit her and she had to scribble it down quickly. She eventually learned good writing takes a lot more time and effort than this. Fortunately, she still loves to write. She's especially lucky because she also loves to travel. She's explored over 45 countries for work and play and can't wait to land in the next new country. It doesn't get any better than writing stories about traveling. Janelle and her husband split their time between a sailboat in Mexico and a house in Colorado.

Adam Turner has been working as a freelance illustrator since 1987. He has illustrated coloring books, puzzle books, magazine articles, game packaging, and children's books. He's loved to draw ever since he picked up his first pencil as a toddler. Instead of doing the usual two-year-old thing of chewing on it or poking his eye out with it, he actually put it on paper and thus began the journey. Adam also loves to travel and has had some crazy adventures. He's swum with crocodiles in the Zambezi, jumped out of a perfectly good airplane, and even fished for piranha in the Amazon. It's a good thing drawing relaxes his nerves! Adam lives in Arizona with his wife and their daughter.

Pack-n-Go Girls Online

Dying to know when the next Pack-n-Go Girls book will be out? Want to learn more Australian slang? Trying to figure out what to pack for your next trip? Looking for cool family travel tips? Interested in some fun learning activities about Australia to use at home or at school while you are reading *Mystery of the Rusty Key*?

- Check out our website:
  www.packngogirls.com
- Follow us on Twitter:
  @packngogirls
- Like us on Facebook:
  facebook.com/packngogirls
- Follow us on Instagram:
  packngogirlsadventures
- Discover great ideas on Pinterest:
  Pack-n-Go Girls

Made in the USA
Coppell, TX
08 November 2021

65427516R00075